TRACTOR MAC

TRACTOR MAC
FAMILY REUNION

Written and illustrated by
BILLY STEERS

FARRAR STRAUS GIROUX • NEW YORK

H ELPING NEIGHBORS BRING in their

harvest was one of Tractor Mac's favorite things to do. The neighboring farm he liked most had train tracks along the fields.

Tractor Mac enjoyed talking with Iron Dave when he stopped sometimes on the tracks.

Sibley the horse was afraid of Iron Dave's noise and steam.

The hissing and clicking made Spartan the colt jump.

"Why do all your cars look alike?" asked Tractor Mac one day.

"I pull different cars on different days," replied Iron Dave.

"I pull stock cars,

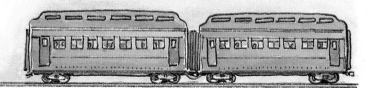

passenger cars,

tank cars,

hopper cars,

and flatcars.

They look alike because they
are all part of the same family."

"There's only one type of me," Tractor Mac said proudly. "I'm the one and only!"

"Ho-ho!" laughed Iron Dave. "Be here tomorrow, Tractor Mac. I will have something to show you."

The next day, as Tractor Mac worked baling hay, he listened for Iron Dave.

What could Iron Dave have to show him besides boxcars carrying freight and hopper cars loaded with coal?

"*WOO-HOOO!*" the whistle blew as Iron Dave huffed up the valley.

Tractor Mac's engine nearly stalled when he saw what the big train pulled: Tractors just like himself loaded on flatcars. Many, many RED tractors!

Iron Dave tooted. Farmer Bill waved. Fetch the dog barked.

"That must be my family!" gasped Tractor Mac.

"You don't even know them," snorted Sibley.

"Aren't we your family?" asked Spartan.

When the day's work was done, Farmer Bill said,
"We need to stop at the tractor dealer for parts on
the way home."

"Sibley! Do you think my family will be there?"
Tractor Mac asked with glee.

"How can they be his family, Uncle Sibley?"
whinnied Spartan.

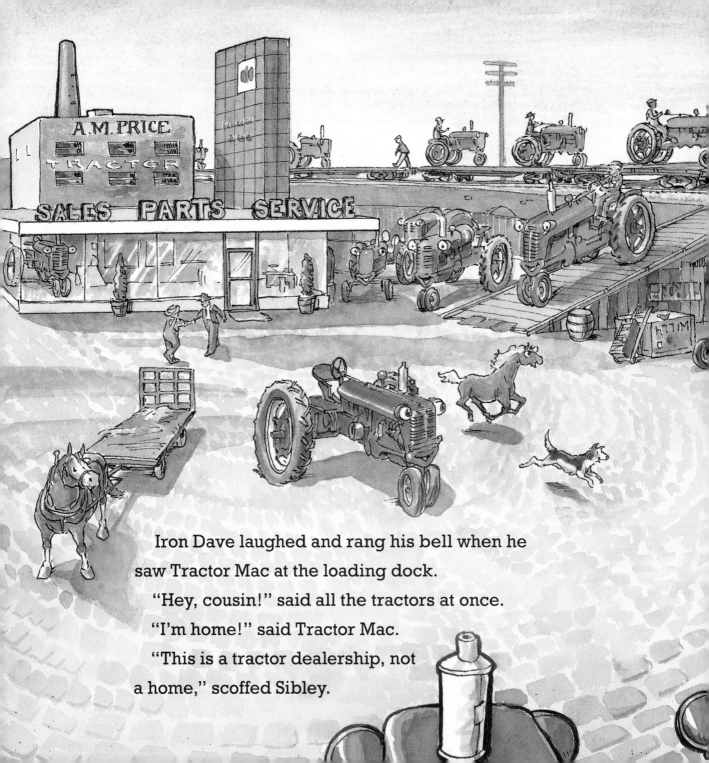

Iron Dave laughed and rang his bell when he
saw Tractor Mac at the loading dock.

"Hey, cousin!" said all the tractors at once.

"I'm home!" said Tractor Mac.

"This is a tractor dealership, not
a home," scoffed Sibley.

There were small row-crop tractors
and tall high-crop tractors.

There were wide tractors

and tractors with strange tanks
to run on different fuels.

There were tractors built for
use in orchards

and tractors built with
continuous tracks.
  They were all *red*,
just like Tractor Mac.

"I want to stay here with my family," said Tractor Mac.
"We're all the same, don't you see?"

"But we are not staying here," chuckled a small-sized tractor.
"This isn't our family," said another tractor.

"We're just here until we get a real farm family of our own," said an older tractor.

"Yes! A farm family that needs us just like yours," agreed a special white-and-red tractor.

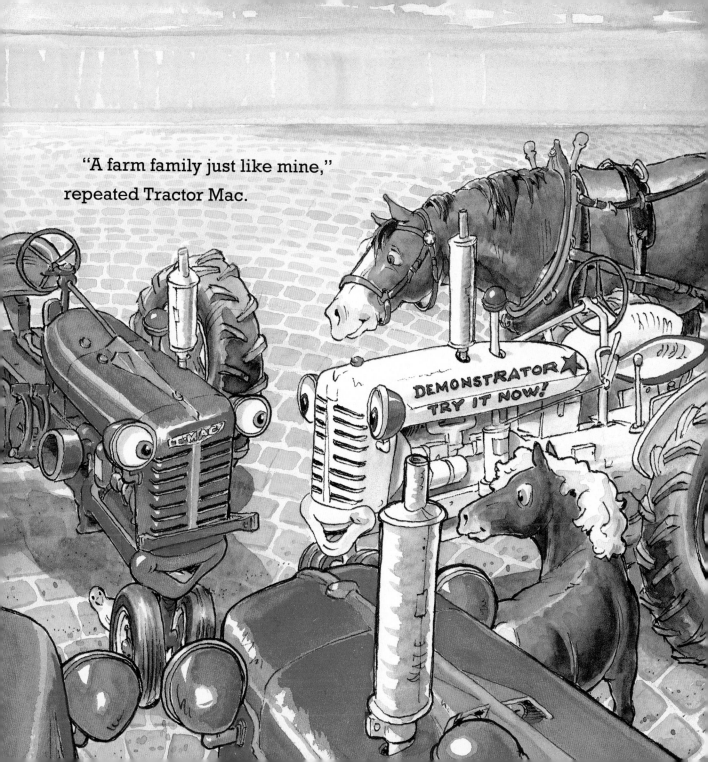

"A farm family just like mine,"
repeated Tractor Mac.

When they arrived home at Stony Meadow Farm, Tractor Mac smiled at Sibley and Spartan. "You were right about family all along," he said with a laugh.

"I'm happy to know there are others out there like me, but . . .

. . . this is my *real* family and I would not trade them for *anything*!"